For Jackson (aka Bam Bam) love Daddy and Grandad Tony Ross

American edition published in 2016 by Andersen Press USA, an imprint of Andersen Press Ltd. www.andersenpressusa.com

First published in Great Britain in 2015 by Andersen Press Ltd., 20 Vauxhall Bridge Road, London SW1V 2SA.

Text copyright © Colin Boyd, 2015. Illustration copyright © Tony Ross, 2015.

Distributed in the United States and Canada by Lerner Publishing Group, Inc. 241 First Avenue North Minneapolis, MN 55401 USA

For reading levels and more information, look up this title at www.lernerbooks.com.

Color separated in Switzerland by Photolitho AG, Zürich. Printed and bound in Malaysia by Tien Wah Press.

Library of Congress Cataloging-in-Publication Data Available.

ISBN: 978-1-5124-0426-5   eBook ISBN: 978-1-5124-0447-0   1-TWP-7/1/15

The Bath Monster

Colin Boyd

Tony Ross

Andersen Press USA

After your bath, do you ever wonder
where the dirty water goes?

Jackson loved all the things that
made him dirty and messy.

His favorite thing was to be outside with his best friend Dexter…

climbing trees...

rolling down hills...

... and playing soccer.

Every night, Jackson's mother would say,

"Look at you!
Go and have a bath now
or the Bath Monster
will come and get you."

Boys and girls everywhere are told about the Bath Monster and his SECOND favorite food: dirty bath water.

Have you ever spotted the water swirl as it goes down the drain?

That's the Bath Monster, slurping the dirty water through his special straw.

Every night, Jackson would have a bath
just to keep the Bath Monster away.

But as he got older, Jackson began to wonder
if there really was a Bath Monster.

One day, when he was out playing soccer with Dexter, Jackson made an epic save and landed in a big, muddy puddle.

Next, the best friends climbed a tree and Jackson fell into an even bigger, muddier puddle.

Then they ran up the biggest hill they could find, and... that's right, they rolled down it into the **biggest,** squelchiest, **muddiest** puddle EVER!

When Jackson got home, his mother said,

"Look at you!"

"Go and have a bath **now** or the
Bath Monster will come and get you."

"NO!" said Jackson.

"I don't believe in bath monsters anymore."

The Bath Monster still believed in Jackson though.

That night, he sat under the bath, waiting for his supper of dirty bath water.

He waited, and waited, and waited, and waited, but Jackson did not have a bath.

Now, if the Bath Monster doesn't get any **dirty bath water,** he **must** eat something.

Everybody knows what his SECOND favorite food is, but not many people know what his absolute, tip-top, FIRST favorite food is...

Me?

That night, Jackson found out.

Dear Mommy
Don't worry
gone to make
Mud Pies
with the
Bath Monster
Love Jackson
xx